The Summit

Paris, France:
West Bank of the Seine

By Edward Roh

RoseDog Books
PITTSBURGH, PENNSYLVANIA 15238

RoseDog Books
585 Alpha Drive, Suite 103
Pittsburgh, PA 15238
Visit our website at *www.rosedogbookstore.com*

ISBN: 979-8-88729-437-7
EISBN: 979-8-88729-937-2

Acknowledgments

With my sincere appreciation, I want to acknowledge the following people who have persevered with me in completing this project and stood by me while I wrote through my times of frustration and elation.

You all deserve much of my admiration for my writing this book.

To my wife, companion, and first-line editor, Kim Roh. You have been a gem in your understanding, patience, and assistance.

Thank you to Dr. Lawrence Waite, who gave me the idea of having Maxwell Perkins as my host in bringing these great writers together and overseeing the project.

To James Fleming, who kindly edited my work and encouraged me.

Also, a dear friend and fellow writer, Chris Kirsh. Thanks, Chris, for your input and encouragement. As with Fitzpatrick and Hemingway, I've enjoyed our conversations about writing, helping me keep my sanity.

May we continue to have many more discussions to come over a pint or two.

I could not have completed this work without all of your support and love.

Edward Roh

Table of Contents

The Preface

As a writer and student of the late nineteenth and early twentieth century authors, I have been intrigued by their skills. Some stories were simplistic; others were more complex.

I wanted to bring together the most prominent writers of that era to discuss their careers and how they composed and approached writing.

I chose to meet at a small café in Paris.

Paris was a destination famous for attracting artisans, musicians, and writers of that period, a place where everyone felt comfortable, familiar, and safe.

I needed someone to oversee this task and settled on Maxwell Perkins from Scribner Brothers Publishing. A Harvard graduate with a degree in economics.

After graduation, Mr. Perkins worked in the news media as an advertising executive for *The New York Times* but chose to publish instead. He was a manager and an editor for new, talented writers, including F. Scott Fitzgerald, Ernest Hemingway, Thomas Wolfe, and others. Most of whom had been rejected by many other publishers. At that time, Scribners Publishing represented only established and elite authors.

He took literary work he deemed rough, disjointed material and helped the writer massage the manuscript into beautiful prose. He recognized and encouraged young writers and became a friend and confidant to all.

His strength as an editor was creative structure. The story might be a great masterpiece but sometimes, needed to be more focused and disciplined with the author's ability to understand the power of the written word.

He knew his authors well and how to bring the best out of them. He was the perfect person to extract talented people's secrets, tragedies, and successes, bring them together and engage in a natural and honest discussion about writing.

His most successful and closest friends and challenges lay with F. Scott Fitzgerald and Ernest Hemingway.

Maxwell was sincere, compassionate, and dedicated to aiding his authors in being successful. Many times, he was more of a friend than an editor.

On occasion, his writers were invited to dinner with his wife and five daughters, perhaps to equal the gender equation of the household.

My manuscript introduces you to the most renowned authors in history. If you have not been exposed to them yet, let me enlighten you about their work; acquaint you with their writing styles; and tell you about the greatest profession of all—being an author.

I imagined what they would have discussed amongst themselves.

It is purely fictional, but I believe it captures the essence and the spirit of each author.

I have read their work, followed the media, and read their biographies. I feel a kinship with their hearts, souls, challenges, personal lives, downturns, and successes.

Each brings wisdom, weakness, strength, and vulnerability to the forefront, with honesty and sincerity. Sometimes with anger, with admiration, and sometimes with remorse.

If you enjoy this book and are intrigued, I suggest you read their work.

Spend a night with these four prestigious authors as they take you through their craft of writing.

Charles Dickens, Feb 7, 1812–June 9, 1870/ 58 yrs.

Ernest Hemingway, July 21, 1899–July 2, 1961/62 yrs.

F. Scott Fitzgerald, Sept 24, 1896–Dec 21, 1940/44 yrs.

O. Henry; William Sydney Porter Sept 11, 1862– June 5, 1910/48 yrs.

Hosted by Maxwell Perkins, Sept 20, 1884– June 17, 1947/63 yrs.

Editor, Scribner Brothers Publishing
Est. 1846
Edward Roh
07.21.2022

Introductions

It was a quiet, Parisian night. A heavy fog had settled in. There was a chill in the air. The sounds of carriage wheels and the clatter of horses' hooves echoed across the cobblestones of Rue Delambre, located on the West bank of the Seine. Gaslights flickered in the dark, dank air.

The atmosphere seemed different as if there was a presence never felt before.

A café door opened without a sound. The shadow of a stately man standing in the doorway was reflected against the dimly lit walls within. He entered the café.

He had been smoking, and the smell followed him into the room. He was wearing a fedora that seemed like an extension of his existence.

He sat at the nearest table by the door. He rested himself, waiting in anticipation of others that would soon be joining.

The door opened a second time.

Maxwell recognized him immediately. There was a fire in his intense, brown eyes; a charm emanated from his presence—a perfect English gentleman.

"Mr. Charles Dickens, I presume?"

"You are correct, sir."

"It is a privilege to be invited to such a gathering of my peers and fellow authors; I would not have missed the opportunity to attend and discuss writing. To share writing techniques and our inspirations for the written word."

Perkins continued, "Please sit where you like. Our other guests will be arriving soon."

A slim, reticent young man, nervous but determined, entered next.

Dickens and Perkins rose to greet him.

"Mr. Dickens, this is William Sydney Porter. Better known as O. Henry."

Dickens bowed. "Your servant, Mr. Porter. I have enjoyed your literature from afar."

O. Henry reciprocated.

"Mr. Dickens, you have always been my most admired author. I tried to emulate you but to no avail. I spent many a day trying to finish your last unfinished book, *The Mystery of Edwin Drood*, without success."

Dickens smiled. "Mr. Porter, nor could I finish it either. Perhaps that's why I left it unfinished."

Laughs and smiles were exchanged.

A well-dressed and pleasant-looking gentleman entered the room next.

"Max, I hope I'm not late. It's always a pleasure to be in your company. I find it intriguing that you should invite me to be a part of such a talented group of authors to discuss writing. Zelda always appreciated your support as my wife. She sends her regards and wishes she could have joined us."

"Gentlemen, my thanks and an honor to be a part of such an elite group of writers."

A chiseled man with white hair, beard, and mustache crossed the threshold—the final of the four invitees entered the room. The door slammed with an abrupt bang!

Maxwell sighed deeply.

"It must be Hemingway," said Maxwell. "Hemingway, you are always the last to enter a room and first and to make the loudest entrance of anyone else."

"You know me well, Perkins. If one cannot enter a room without a flare of greatness, why enter it at all?"

He shook Maxwell's hand with a firm grip and a smile. "Thanks for inviting me. I look forward to a great and glorious conversation."

Max smiled.

"Gentlemen," said Maxwell, "what I want to do this evening is to have you share the experience of writing. Your thoughts; what drove you to write, your challenges, disappointments; to exchange thoughts, ideas, successes, and failures."

Motivations

"What motivated you to write and be successful? Was it from personal experience, the people you knew, your background, observing the times you were in, your education, lack of it, or just street smarts? Why were you compelled to write at all?

"Porter, I'll begin with you. You had opportunities to write stories of the wealthy and the young who progressed to rise into successful careers and a life of financial security. Yet you tended to write of a less successful class of people."

O. Henry frowned, then smiled. "You can address me with my first name. You can call me Will."

"A well-asked question, Mr. Perkins.

"I saw no story to write for those people because they came from a world where fate had already been destined for them; they would live in total happiness and comfort. I saw no challenges or hardships before them. There was no story to write.

"My reflections were about the souls who were beaten down, the poor and downtrodden, still believing in a world that was kind and never lost trust in life; their destiny was to find a place in a world of love, providence, and faith, trusting in compassion and innocent love to make their dreams and desires come true. Never doubting life would turn out for the best.

"I wrote many stories with twists and turns. Some were tragic; some were magic. I wrote with humor and compassion and hopes of a happy ending. I enjoyed laughter, delighting in dreams coming true, and facing adversity, but never at the cost of disappointment to any of my characters."

O. Henry went quiet.

Dickens responded.

"Bravo, O. Henry! Well taken.

"You have a unique style of taking verse with a few twists and turns, making it into a beautiful story. I love your plots that always keep it interesting and engaging, concluding with an ending clear and concise. I feel the fondness for your characters as you gently bring their stories to a glorious conclusion.

"Good writing is honest and engaging. The simplicity of your manuscripts makes them easy to read and comprehend. It engages the reader to the point that you want to finish it without interruption.

"I commend you on your tenacity and persistence."

Max retook the floor.

"There will be much more time for discussion as the night wears on.

"Fitzgerald, in your first novel, *This Side of Paradise*, I was taken by your prose. Your style intrigued me.

"Hemingway, your stories were engaging. The manuscripts reverberated on the edge of pain, emotion, and a sense of urgency. The endings were sometimes abrupt but effective.

"Can you elaborate on your writing genre and connection with the readers?"

Hemingway bowed.

"Mr. Fitzgerald, since you are my senior, I acquiesce. Do take the floor first, sir."

"Mr. Hemingway, thank you, sir. I shall take it.

"My desire to write came from many places. I grew up in a well-to-do neighborhood. Not rich, but indeed not poor. I longed for the privileges of the families that touched mine. I was never envious but curious. What magic must be inside those protected walls? What was I missing?"

"It was a curiosity that haunted me all of my life. It was my destiny to live it and define it.

"I saw the tragedy of being able to live a comfortable life but never experiencing the life beyond my own boundaries.

"I wrote about it. My characters being confident, yet vulnerable.

"I lived outside of my imagination and in it.

"I realized great success was no success at all—a facade, a hiding place to shadow the walls of insecurity.

"A place where we all live vicariously and then soon disappear.

"My characters reflected it. They were bold, pompous, and brave, but weak.

"I created from the world I lived in—my imagination."

"What motivated me to write?"

"Zelda was my life and existed to make me whole.

"I could not have written without her.

"Society and the characters of my stories made my dreams real. I tried to find a place in a world that did not exist.

"I believed my short stories and novella surpassed my novels, but few have ever explored them.

"I finally found my gift in the last novel that I never got to finish. *The Last Tycoon*."

"Mr. Hemingway, I give the floor back to you."

Hemingway began.

"We are of the same world, different lives. "I'll not go into detail but say I desired to write. I was challenged to write."

"Yes, Max. I always looked at life from a different view.

"I wasn't cruel, just realistic.

"I hated war; I hated killing.

"My stories and the people were real. It's what I experienced in life and shared with the world.

"From gored toreadors in Spain to dying soldiers in the fields of battle to safaris in the jungle. Man against beast.

"Reflections of distrust and deception in a relationship.

"I enjoyed and employed my characters. Sometimes it may have seemed graphic. Life is never simple or a fairy tale. I wrote about life, loving, living, sacrifice, and dying.

There is nothing nobler than dying for a cause. That was my inspiration."

Maxwell responded. "Thanks, Hemingway. Well noted.

"Mr. Dickens, we have yet to address your motivation for writing."

"I'm patient, Mr. Perkins, and am willing to share my absorption into the literary world.

"My stories encompass the desire to write with those in the room.

"Writing is complex. Everyone can write, but not everyone can be an author. I want to make that clear. In this century, many should have chosen to be satisfied with being just a writer and not an author.

"My repast was served with a great deal of experience and observation. Characters that reflect the frailties of human nature. Many were cruel, many were kind, and many were greedy. But most of all, they reflected the heart of humankind.

"We all have a bit of Scrooge and a bit of Tiny Tim in all of us."

"We have ghosts that haunt us, and try to hide from them. At the same time, we are surrounded by guardian angels that protect us.

"That's what makes us human. My characters were real, if not in life perhaps, but in spirit.

"Growing up, I knew all of my characters as real people. I chose to bring out the best and sometimes the worst in them. I knew their fallibilities but never fed on their maliciousness or harshness. Sometimes laughable, sometimes tragic; in the end, they all had to realize what they had become and change—or be consumed by life.

"Writing was my way to help people see reality. It was a choice."

Max proceeded. But not before lighting another cigarette.

"There seems to be a common thread amongst you. Your mutual interest and desire to write respectfully with full resolve resounds throughout your writings."

Development

"Did character development drive you, or was it the story?

"What about character interaction? Who dominated your manuscripts? The male or the female.

"What did each bring to the table? Why?"

"I shall take that one first," said O. Henry. "If no one objects?"

"Away with it then, Will."

It was Hemingway. "Enlighten us."

All nodded.

"As you all know, I wrote for the *Houston Chronicle* in my earlier years. Writing for the press made me write short and to the point. A bit irrelevant, but most of us here did the same.

"I also worked at a bank in Austin, where I was accused, tried, and convicted of embezzlement. Later I was acquitted of all charges but spent three years in prison. I left behind a sick wife and a small child.

"It changed me. To support my daughter, I started writing short stories and selling them under the name of O. Henry to protect my daughter from shame and protect my reputation.

"Stories came from inmates that suffered the same existence as I. They told me stories of their lives and their families.

"My first works were versed in their tragedies. I saw their sincerity and heartbreak. I also saw the opportunity to right the wrongs—even if just in a story.

"My motivation came from both the story and the characters. My characters were a mix of fact and fiction. It taught me that being poor was not a shame but a virtue.

"There is no division between the story and character."

"There could be no story without both a man and a woman. God never meant for us to be separated. Each had an essential part to perform. They contributed equally.

"I lost my wife to consumption, but her soul still echoes in all I write.

"I made enough money to support my child. That was all I asked.

Perkins interacted, "Humbling, Will. I appreciate your candor.

"Fitzgerald, you have a lot on your plate to share. I have known you for many years. Please expound your opinion."

"Maxwell, you are so kind as to let me go next. You know me for my shortcomings, triumphs, and disappointments I left with you. I am indebted to you.

"Forgive me for my weaknesses, and thank you for my successes. In addition to being a great editor, you have always been a friend."

He bowed. Perkins returned the bow.

"As my dear friend Hemingway has repeatedly told me, my weakness and strength came from my only true love, Zelda.

"Her passion for life and her effervescence flowed through me like a fountain.

"The pen wrote as if I was not even attached to it. My stories wrote themselves.

"I developed my characters based on our own insecure lives.

"In Jay Gatsby, there was a dreamer and part of me of fulfilling my desires.

"Nick Carroway, the neighbor next door, was from Minnesota, where I was born and raised. He was another part of me. An observer of aspirations, a witness to the disaster of dreams that went wrong.

"Daisy Buchanan, a beautiful woman who once scorned Jay and proceeded to marry into money, her passion for living in luxury."

"Tom Buchanan, her husband, gave her everything she wanted. All except love.

"Myrtle Wilson and her partner, George Wilson, lived a poor existence. A car mechanic in a decrepit neighborhood who adored her but could only give her love with dirty hands. She longed for better but had to live with what she had been given.

"Tom Buchanan gave her what she desired.

"Does that scenario tell you anything about my writing? The story and how the characters intertwined?

"I could neither write nor create without my affection and care for both.

"The inspiration came from Zelda.

"My brief writing career echoed all of the emotions that I've mentioned.

"And, Mr. Hemingway, that was how I wrote, sir."

Hemingway remained silent.

"Mr. Dickens, you have been the most prolific. It seems you are the artist of creating people with names that still linger at the tip of our tongues.

"The names. Where did they come from, and why does a name like 'Scrooge' resound in the minds of even children?

"Your humor was immense. Your use of tragedy and despair bled our hearts.

"Sometimes, even in your endings, your tragedies seemed to let us rest at peace.

"How did your character development and the story meet?

"Your heart. Please, sir?"

With dignity, Dickens began.

"You ask much of me, Mr. Perkins.

"My beginning was humble. My journey was long."

"I would not change a single step of the path through the life that I have traversed. It was what made me the author that I was.

"You cannot write anything in the present without the history of the past.

"As with you, Mr. Porter, my life was simple.

"I admire you, your perseverance and talent.

"My most lucid memories started when I was three years old. I recall voices and people who came and went, always leaving me with a distinct curiosity about them. Where did they come from; where did they go? Were they like me?

"My mother and father bickered often.

"My father was incarcerated in a debtor's prison when I was twelve. I was apprenticed to a boot blackening factory in London.

"I worked twelve-hour days, seldom had enough to eat, and wore my only clothes—nothing but mere rags to keep the cold and dampness away.

"I memorized the people and emotions around me. You ask where my imagination came from? It came from childhood, sometimes harsh but compassionate. I was forced to accept and understand the world as it was.

"All of the characters came from my background. I was an observer of life in the audience of good theater.

"My stories were the prominent feature. I backfilled them with the colorful characters I created.

"I was informed that I have brought into existence over

1,500 characters within the pages of my manuscripts.

"All of my books incorporated men and women, equally prominent in the story."

"The stories made the adventure; the characters are what colored them. From Scrooge to Bob Cratchit, Jacob Marley, Tiny Tim, Uriah Heep, and Miss Haversham.

"From Little Nell, Fezziwig, David Copperfield, Mrs. Cratchit, and more.

"If the current reader does not know these wonderful people, I suggest you read some of my literature.

"I rest my case."

Maxwell responded. "Well taken, Mr. Dickens. And explained.

"Mr. Hemingway, the air appears open for you to tell us about your writing."

"As always, Maxwell, you have saved the best for last."

A broad, bodacious smile covered his face.

"I shall go into as much detail as you wish.

"Your question is a double-edged sword, sir: the story or the characters. They cannot be separated. I wrote from the standpoint of what I experienced. The story outlined the characters, and the characters made the story.

"Gender had nothing to do with the story. All characters played their part.

"As a writer, I saw no differentiation between men and women. I treated my characters with equality, based on the role they played.

"My desire was to write a damn good story. All of my people counted.

"The prose needed to be simple and direct without clutter. Critics said I called it the *iceberg theory*.

"What lies below the surface need not be seen. They are

the underpinnings of emotions that write the story. The words should be to the point. Fewer words and more emotion allow the reader to feel the raw, unabated truth. Simplistic and straightforward."

"A book should reflect humanity. It's about self-respect, the vulnerability of frailties and failures, making mistakes, and acknowledging that fact.

"You need to forgive yourself and others; then move on without rage or regret.

"I wrote from my heart. I served as an ambulance driver for the Red Cross in times of war, retrieving the dead and rescuing the wounded. I learned much from that experience.

"I addressed death often in my stories. There is no glory in dying. Accept it as a fact and with dignity.

"Live life with fervor and passion. Live it with honor and pride. Experience as much as possible; challenge your dreams in the face of adversity. When young, we do not see death as an option. Only a threat; never a reality.

"That is how I wrote. And how I lived."

It was Maxwell.

"Thank you, Hemingway. You have always written on the edge, and it paid off by receiving a Pulitzer Prize for fiction in 1953 for 'The Old Man in the Sea' and the Nobel Peace prize for all of your writings in 1954."

Perkins took a long draw of his cigarette. Then another, and exhaled.

Observations

"I have a few other questions before the sun rises. But first, I want to know your observations of other writers; past, present, and future.

"Be honest. Be blunt. This is where we begin to discuss writing.

"Hemingway, you are bold; please begin."

With much reflection, he began.

"One thing that has me perplexed. If I were alive today, could I write and relate to today's readers?

"Life has changed so much. Things move so quickly now; it would be hard to write a classical novel.

"There is still war, hunger, emotion, trauma, and drama.

"The story would still be about hardships. Life, death, war, existence, persecution. That hasn't changed."

"I agree, Hemingway." It was O. Henry. "Even my stories, I think, would work today. Times have progressed. But the simplicity of our lives no longer exists.

"Still, I think the formula would work.

"What people call technology changes life and creativity. Nostalgia, clinging on to old memories, has disappeared.

"Hearts are still human; human frailties exist. Souls are lost and won every day. Love and compassion still exist. No matter what era you wrote in, some things are unchanging.

"Books aren't as important today as they were in our time.

To enjoy a good romance, a comedy, or an adventure, we needed to settle down with a book and read it slowly, in candlelight, immersing ourselves in the characters and plot as it evolved."

"We hated to see them come to an end because the characters became our friends and companions.

"We cried with them. Sometimes they were vile, and we detested them. Some we loved, and they became our heroes and heroines; our idols. We couldn't wait for the next chapter to begin.

"On occasion, I would finish a chapter and put the book back on the shelf to contemplate what would happen next and try not to read it again for a whole week, just to relive what I had read and anticipate the next adventure before refreshing my relationship with old friends and new acquaintances and the next experience.

"I took time to absorb the story.

"I am disappointed with literature today. Few writers take the agonizing time like we did to savor every word written; to rewrite until you've found the perfect adjective and description of the character or event.

"Books are published by the thousands today; sold, sometimes read, and discarded soon thereafter.

"Books and time created libraries. I don't recall a household without a library or at least a reading room. Stories were a wonder and a great treasure. The library was the heart of a home.

"As for future writers and authors, I hope the glimpse of our past reflects upon their minds and influences them to write for the love of writing—not fame, fortune, or glory. Because that is an illusion.

"Writing comes from the heart, not the pocketbook. People will remember you for your writing—not how popular you were. Fame comes well after your death."

Dickens spoke up. "Gentlemen, I fear you are too delusional. Optimistic, but delusional."

"Our time has come and gone. I would not even contemplate writing in this new world or the future.

"We were great and illustrious writers in our time. Let it go at that.

"*A Tale of Two Cities, Dombey and Sons, Great Expectations, Our Mutual Friend, The Old Curiosity Shop.*

"Does that mean much to anyone today?

"Probably not. I wrote of a past era. One that really existed. A time and stories that could never be replicated.

"My prose was elaborate and visual.

"I spent hours creating those scenarios. That, my friends, was my reality.

"I have been told if I wrote with such clarity and honesty today, my books would have never been published.

"I'm satisfied with my place in literary history, and there I shall remain.

"Hemingway, your sense of valor and fiction surpassed mine.

"My favorite was *The Old man and the Sea.*

"The coming together of life, grabbing the last victory, yet simultaneously experiencing the final loss with dignity."

"No one except another writer could appreciate it. It is my favorite tribute to literary immortality.

"I must agree with Dickens." Fitzgerald chimed in. "My stories came from what now is a quiet world."

"A society locked in self-preservation. Existing on a thread and a misguided allusion of self-importance, with no morals or roots, just a world that you think owes you everything because of who you were.

"The 'jazz era,' as they called it.

"No, I could not write in this world today. I could not write with the fervor and compassion I did in the '20s.

"The decadence and shamelessness scandal of today's world is even worse. At least, there was a sense of honor and dignity in our time.

"I choose not to re-enter this world of literature.

"As with Dickens, I take my place in the literary history of an era gone by."

Challenges

Perkins interrupted, "Challenges, gentlemen. Let's talk about challenges."

Fitzgerald seemed agitated: "Be more direct, Max.

"Are you talking about personal challenges? What challenges; in the vernacular of creativity? What challenges do you wish to address?

"Are you addressing obstacles, roadblocks, writer's block, what the readers anticipated, or what we expected from ourselves? What was the editor looking for in our next novel? Or all of it?"

"Be more specific. My misunderstanding of the question grows.

Perkins answered with his normal half grin and half frown, showing no sign of emotion.

"All of it."

Fitzgerald stewed a bit and looked at the others.

All were silent. There was no eye contact.

It was a sensitive subject.

The room went silent for what seemed like an eternity.

Each author took time to reflect.

Dickens came forth first.

"That is a broad question, sir.

"Mr. Perkins; it is not that we are trying to deflect your pertinent questions. As famous writers, people sometimes forget we are human as well."

"Thanks, Dickens," responded Hemingway. "People liked to think we lived a glamorous and wonderful life. Weakness and virtue have no place in the public's mind of an author."

"In the middle of myth is the harsh reality of life, balancing sanity, fiction, family, fame, and the truth. I'll not go into my personal life.

"Many have gone there before. I have nothing to say, but it was my private life. Not my professional life, and no one has a right to examine it. I lived it every day.

"If it's my professional life, I will talk about it all day and night. I loved sitting in a café here in Paris with my friend, Fitzgerald. We drank too much, sang too much, argued too much, but relished our conversations about writing, comparing notes, bragging, and being our pompous selves.

"Fitzgerald, you are still my favorite author. I chide you in earnest. You were one of the greatest writers of our time. Critics were hard on you, but your words rang true. I wish you had written more.

"I enjoyed your unfinished book, *The Last Tycoon*. We needed more.

"It was best you had ever written."

"Thank you, Hemingway. It is one of the reasons I wanted to return tonight; to discuss those very things. And address that."

Fitzgerald smiled. "I also enjoyed our conversations in those days. It was always better than writing."

"Writing was exhausting and difficult.

"We took our time to create and even more time to rewrite."

Dickens signed in.

"I also had my cronies, especially playwright and author Wilkie Collins. We would while away the hours, sharing stories, tipping a pint or two at a local pub, and discussing writing and technique."

O. Henry spoke up. "I think we are all in agreement. We've all found ourselves in some kind of confinement or prison, if you will, when writing.

"We've all had our adversities and skeletons in the closet. Did they affect how we wrote?

"Of course, they did, but the bottom line is not who we were, but who our characters and stories were.

"Too much time was wasted trying to find out about our private lives. That's why I wrote under a pen name and chose to stay anonymous.

"I think it's worse today than it ever was in our time.

Perkins spoke.

"Well-taken points, gentlemen. I believe you have answered a critical question tonight. I meant not to probe; I wanted your reaction to public opinion and personal exposure."

Roadblocks

"Let's touch areas outside of our private and public lives.

"I detected some resistance to a few of my chosen words; perhaps the words 'writer's block and roadblocks' seem to be a sensitive subject.

"I don't mean to bring up an issue, but it's out there. Any comments, or would you like to refrain from that subject as well?"

Hemingway and Fitzgerald exchanged glances and smiled.

"Hemingway, my friend, I shall approach that subject first," began Fitzgerald.

"You have brought up a very sensitive issue. As a writer, this is the most unspoken taboo of all. The loss of the ability to write. The ability not to be creative is devastating.

"Nothing is worse than to look at an empty page for hours without a sentence being created; it is a nightmare. The harder you try, the deeper the chasm becomes.

"You sink into an abysmal depression. Nights without sleep, angst, and drunkenness become your sole companions.

"It's a hole that only you understand and only you can pull yourself out of that pit. Time heals all issues, but in the meantime, you're living in purgatory between heaven and hell thinking, 'can I or will I' ever write again?

"And yes. If you are a writer, a time will come when it will happen.

"I wrote only four novels in my short writing career. Only

four. I wrote short stories as well but stumbled in finishing any more. I ended up as a screenwriter hack in Hollywood to take care of Zelda.

"The reasons are many for writer's block. If I knew the answer to why, I could have solved many more complex issues."

"Fitzgerald is right." It was Hemingway. "It was six years of hell before I wrote my next relevant novel. Short stories filled the void.

"I finally resolved to write at least one coherent sentence a day.

"In between, I struggled and even wrote a book that the critics panned and said my career was over. They went back to my previous work and condemned those as well.

"They said my writing was overrated and reckless.

"My last novel proved them wrong."

Next was Dickens.

"The term echoes in my mind. I do not quite understand as it was not terminology that I recognized. Not being able to write, I understand. Yes.

"There were times that I found it confounding. But I worked through it. I had my private studio at Gad's House, where no one was entitled to enter but myself.

"Yes. There were periods of non-productivity, but I worked my way through it. I did not know the term, 'writer's block.'

"Thank God I didn't."

O. Henry joined in. "I never experienced a block. My mind was always on fire, and the stories never stopped coming.

Laughingly he replied, "But I died when I was forty-eight."

All had a hardy laugh.

Perkins was ready to move on. "What was your greatest obstacle as a writer?"

Dickens began the discussion. "Writing is a lonely occupation. You confine yourself to a small room with only a pen, a pad, your ideas, and yourself."

"You are isolated in a world of your own. There is no one to bounce ideas off. You write in the hope that the story is interesting, fulfilling, and good enough to publish and for the public to enjoy.

"One of the most difficult things is shutting yourself off from your family, friends, and the rest of humanity. To write, you must be disciplined and focused.

"That is a very difficult thing to do. That's why, as writers, we seek the attention of other writers; to protect our sanity and assure ourselves we are worthy of each other's work."

"Dickens is right," stated Hemingway. "As writers, we fade from the real world into fantasy and fiction. I believe we are just a little left of center.

"We live in a different world that sometimes takes us astray. Some call us eccentric, or distant, not knowing reality from fiction.

"That's what writers do; it keeps us one step ahead of boredom and the mundane. We are what people want us to be and what we would like to be.

"Bold, daring, brave, and adventurous. We made life stand out from their everyday existence.

"People want to live in our make-believe world, visualizing that it's their world too, hoping that it is real; fantasizing that this is who we are and who they want to become.

"We are judged and tried by what we write. Yes, there is great truth in our creations, and they are a part of our ego and id, but it's fantasy, and sometimes even we get caught up in what we write."

Fitzgerald was the next to comment.

"We lived, agonized, and became a part of our own created characters. For the most part, it was our escape from reality."

O. Henry was last to speak.

"We avoided our human inadequacies by writing. It kept us from having to live the sad life we are exposed to every day.

"People lived vicariously through our works."

Distractions

Hemingway took the floor. "Perkins, a better question might be, what were our distractions and our distraught?"

Maxwell smiled. "Do tell."

It seemed to have touched a nerve of true discomfort. Each had demons from the past that genuinely did challenge and bother them.

Insecurities, doubt, fear of failure, or fear of success: habits that let them hide their iniquities.

Fitzgerald was a writing phenomenon with his first book. He had reservations, and fear, wondering if he could repeat it.

Hemingway was far from being a loved author. He was mostly recognized as a "man's" author. He wrote from the heart. Damn, if it mattered to him what the reader wanted or thought. It was his story. Take it or leave it.

O. Henry never knew success until his death. He wrote with his heart. It was only after his death did the sales of his book rise.

Dickens never looked at writing as a success or failure. He could only create a dynamic story capturing the hearts and minds of the reader, whoever that might be. Success to him was money enough to feed his family.

It was Hemingway. "Let's talk about distractions and our distraught."

Maxwell smiled and spoke up. "Let's discuss distraught and distraction further, then."

Fitzgerald responded.

"There are roadblocks. If you've never been an author, let alone a writer. In our world, our stories and verses matter."

"Our characters are real. They exist for a purpose. Redline a paragraph or ghost a character; let me know why.

"In our mind, each word we write has a meaning to the end.

"If you disrupt my thought process, then we have to talk.

"Maxwell, you know better than any of us as your hands were full with all of us."

He continued, "I think we all know, never doubt your editor. You make us all successful but explain your logic. If you are ghosting my characters or redlining copy, you are messing with our creativity."

He smiled. "I'm done, sir."

Everyone exploded in laughter at Fitzgerald's outburst, as did Maxwell.

"Somehow, I thought you would be the quiet one in the group. You, it seems, have become the rogue." Maxwell smiled.

Fitzgerald blushed. Another loud laugh arose from those present.

Writing Habits

"Let's go another direction then. Tell me about your writing habits. Do you outline the storyline, start with a beginning and an end, and fill in from there? Or do you freelance, letting the story develop as your characters evolve?

"Are you disciplined to write a certain amount every day, or write as the process dictates to you?"

Hemingway went first.

"My stories come fully loaded.

"I know the plot and the characters before I write and where they will finish up.

"My approach is to be raw and impactful. Know the character from the beginning, and you cannot go wrong. You either hate them or love them. There's no in-between. You know at the very beginning who is the antagonist and protagonist.

"Other characters come into play, but they are simply the pawns that make the story progress.

"I do not use an outline as this would make writing more difficult.

"When I write, I have the complete story in mind and proceed, from start to finish. I take notes as I sometimes lose track of ideas. You needed to.

"Yes, sometimes my secondary characters surprised me, but I don't let them upset the flow of the story or my thought process. They can add to the nourishment of the plot but never steal the role of my main characters.

"I tried to write at least a thousand words a day. Many a day, I would take my Remington typewriter, a ream of paper, and a pen and pad with me to Sloppy Joe's in the Florida Keys, where I lived and wrote until noon, and then enjoy a few cups with everyone."

"It was comforting to hear the 'clink' of beer glasses, the meaningless bar banter around me, and the bravado of friends and patrons.

"Sometimes they would feed me a line or an idea that would add to my prose as I worked or for future reference.

"Yes. There were times I needed my privacy as well."

Fitzgerald was next.

"Hemingway, we are so far apart in preparation.

"I could not write in such an environment. I needed peace and tranquility.

"Structure is everything, Maxwell.

"I start with a concept and an outline. Otherwise, how do you keep track of the flow of the story?

"As with Hemingway, I have my heroes and villains, but I allow them to progress, to show their humor, love, remorse, and weaknesses.

"As I've said before, they make it simple for me. I let them write the story and their epitaph.

"When I write, I have an outline and a preconceived idea as to how it will end. I don't know precisely how it will end, but I know when it will end. It's the journey that dictates the story.

"Unlike Hemingway, I have no subordinate actors. All are equal and contribute to the story, enhancing the main characters or bringing out their weaknesses.

"My stories begin aloof. Let the reader deduce the character of my subjects; let them grow and become a person people you either love or hate. Sooner or later, the true self shows through. Let them have dreams, ambitions, and desires. You will get to know them soon enough. I let the reader interpret these people and determine their contribution and worth.

"I write daily, even if it's but a few lines. As we discussed, writer's block is hell; you can only overcome it if you write just a few words daily."

O. Henry stood up, stretched, and began his oratory.

"You all humble me. I was raised by my aunt and tutored at home. I had little contact with other children and relied on my auntie to teach me the world. I enjoyed literature and reading classics. That is how I became enamored with Dickens's books.

"I wrote short stories that did not need much research. My stories were short and simple. That did not lessen their value. Just the length of the stories.

"Throughout my life, words were valuable. I carried a dictionary with me no matter where I went. Even in prison.

"I did not create outlines. I kept notebooks. My stories were simple. Sometimes I could write them within a day. Others could take a little longer.

"I tried to keep my characters simple and never turn anyone into a villain.

"Everyone is a reflection of ourselves.

"There were no bad people. Only victims.

"I saw and wrote about the simple attributes of mankind. There is no room for vindictiveness in this world, only forgiveness and the simple love for each other.

Everyone at the table squirmed, uncomfortable.

Dickens was the last to contribute.

"Mr. Porter, O. Henry; you are the purest writer of all of us. You deserve credit and our admiration."

"Sometimes, as successful writers, we lose track of humanity and what writing is all about. Thank you for the sobering reminder. It will be hard to follow up on your observations.

"Richness of character, the story—all have to come together for a compelling story and make it meaningful. You have made it simple and to the point.

"My stories were rich in description. Each character and each action had to be precise to lead to the next emotion and reaction.

"As with you, O. Henry, words were important to me. I wanted to make each word ring true to the plot. My saddest story was *The Old Curiosity Shop*. One of my few tragedies.

"Mr. Perkins, I could only capture my stories in my day using pen and pad.

"I wrote just about every day. Notes and imagination were my only tools, but I had one tool that few writers have today.

"I serialized my stories, writing one or two chapters a week. I could send it off for printing and await feedback from my readers on how to proceed with the story.

"Without that input, I don't know if the written books would have turned out to be the same.

"I owe a lot of gratitude to those who religiously read my short stories and helped me turn them into successful novels.

"Sometimes, I am saddened to say I wrote just to pay the bills and raise my family. I was fortunate to have the ability to write stories that people enjoyed."

Maxwell commented. "Well taken, and I appreciate your honesty."

Success

"This leads me to the next question.

"What is your perception of success; did you accomplish your goals?"

O. Henry responded, "I wrote and sold my stories to support my family as best I could. I never had a thought of glory or fame.

"I believe my gratification was to write, and yes, I was successful.

"My failure was in being a father and a husband. It was not of my choosing; it occurred.

"Writing enabled me to pay bills and support my daughter. We were estranged but found our way back into each other's lives.

"I never felt the humiliation of being critiqued or judged by the public.

"Questions and inquiries inundated my editor.

"'Who is O. Henry? He has compassion that reflects not a man but a woman's sensitivity. Can you send a photo of this writer?'

"I threatened my publisher never to reveal my identity.

"It saved me a great deal of inconsequential fame and gave me anonymity. I was never wealthy, but we paid the bills and were happy.

"I, too, had my ghosts, but we were happy. That to me equates to success.

From Dickens: "I've not seen or heard success so eloquently expressed. Thank you."

Maxwell moved forward.

"Fitzgerald, let's hear from you."

"Success is a relative and broad term, Mr. Perkins.

"Are we speaking of financial gain, respect, personal satisfaction, completion of a story?"

Maxwell responded.

"I'm asking you the question. What do you feel is a success? Have you attained what you wanted to?"

A great and serious pause went by.

"I have attained many. I need not go into that. I have also left many tasks uncompleted. "That is the best way that I can answer that question."

He said no more. With some embarrassing silence and discomfort, Hemingway picked up the slack.

"As a writer, but mostly as a human being, I don't think we ever feel successful. When you feel you have accomplished something, doubt settles in, and you think, I could have done better.

"Success has many layers.

"Professional accomplishments are wonderful; there is a rush of finishing a book and seeing it in print; the accolades of the critics and readers.

"Then you start looking for the next challenge.

"We write because that's our profession. Financially, we need to pay our bills, but it's not a success factor.

"Personal challenges come into play as well. Maybe sometimes we take ourselves too seriously. As authors, that is the damn curse we are challenged with daily.

"Speaking for myself, I think writers are more paranoid than anyone else. We look for approval and admiration but question it when it comes.

"Because of that, our health and personal relationships suffer. I wish to God it was not so, but therein lies the truth, damn it!

"I'm being honest, Maxwell. I've never hidden anything from you."

Perkins smiled.

"Mr. Hemingway, you have been pompous, a bully, and an ass, but you have always spoken straightforward, concise, and honest. I respect your brevity."

Hemingway laughed. "Thank you."

"And Thank you, sir." Maxwell laughed, and so did everyone else in the room.

Perkins said, "Dickens, it's up to you to carry the caboose."

"Success is an illusion. The word never fit into my vocabulary, sir. Today's success is tomorrow's failure.

"Hard work and tedious dedication are the only way to accomplish your goals. Did I become successful?

"In those terms? I would say yes.

"Always remember; never trust in your yesterday or the now, but only in tomorrow. The best is yet to come.

Perkins concluded.

"Well taken, all of you. I do not mean to offend or invade your privacy; just a means of capturing your creativity for prosperity and advice for future writers who may soon face the same challenges that you did."

Failures

"I have but a few more questions. Bear with me because I feel they are important factors in our journey tonight.

"As an author, what weighed heaviest on your mind: fear of failure, fear of success?

"Take me into your world."

"An interesting question, Mr. Perkins." It was Dickens.

"I never gave it a thought. Writing comes from creativity. It never weighed on my mind. I took the story to where it needed to go. Oh, I relied on feedback and suggestions from some of my peers and readers.

"But did I fear success or failure?

"I suppose in the back of my mind, I did. But I was always ahead of myself, thinking of the next chapter or the next book.

"I did not let fame or fortune dictate my life at the time; I had neither.

"It was an emotion that didn't bother me.

"I think it was O. Henry that said, 'Fame comes when you're dead, and fortune is an illusion.'"

O. Henry responded.

"Mr. Dickens, we are of the old school. I, too, never gave it a second thought. "Yes, my concern was that each story would be embraced by my readers. The biggest worry was making enough money to keep me in writing supplies and raising my daughter.

"I had plenty of stories to write and never let critics bother me. The only ones I cared about were my readers and the twist and turns of the next story."

"As Dickens says, it was the story that counted; I never second-guessed my work as a good book writes itself. I'm just along for the ride; to carry the wonder of the words forward."

Sitting at the table, hands folded, Fitzgerald listened and smiled. He replied, "Gentlemen, thank you for your insight. I admire your dedication to your work, and yes, I believe you lived in a little bit of a different circumstance.

"Hemingway and I lived in a world of critics, ready to displace you. If your first or even the second book was successful, they were anxious to read the next one, so they could critique and prove to the public that the first few books were a fluke.

"Maxwell, I believe your question is valid. To me, fear of success and failure are the same.

"As with Dickens and O. Henry, I enjoyed writing my stories and admired my readers because, no matter what a critic may essay, it is truly in the hands of the public. They drive the success or the failure of a book.

"Without the strength of a great editor such as Maxwell, as a writer, you can be eaten by the critics who can tear you apart like piranhas.

"Success is a rush you feel when you've finished a story, and it is accepted as a glorious work of literature, but elation is short-lived. There is another side of success.

"Failure.

"Success is short-lived. Failure is ever present, waiting like a great ghost, a pit ready to pull you down into obscurity.

"Maxwell, I was driven by both fear of success and failure."

Hemingway listened, frowned, and observed, "A healthy question for anyone who has written. You are always only as good as your last manuscript. It can be a classic, and in doing so, you set yourself up for disappointment and failure.

"Understand, each book is a world within itself. Every book and every short story must be different. Sometimes to the point of disappointment by some readers, but a new adventure for others.

"You can never write the same story twice. I don't think some people realize that.

"It's called talent and creativity. Sometimes I didn't like some of my stories as much as others, but they were all my family.

"If you are so mundane to go to work each day, never wavering, eat the same meals every day, and go through the same routine year after year, you are not living, but merely existing.

"That is why we as writers are embraced.

"Each story is one within itself. Sometimes variety brings a curse upon itself.

"I have never had a fear of success. Only the fear of disappointment. Is that the same as fear of failure?

"No. Hardly. Disappointment comes from those who don't understand your motive or your spirit and soul.

"As with Fitzgerald, that's what destroys your energy and drive. If I had to write the same story, with the same ending every time, I'd rather not write."

Legacy

Maxwell took a moment to reflect.

"I think this is the most powerful question we have addressed tonight.

"I'll leave it at that.

"The last question of this special evening.

"How do you want your readers to remember your legacy? What do you want them to remember as your final epitaph?"

Hemingway: "Bold, brazen, and a bull. I am a man of few words in my writing, but each syllable is a reflection of my soul.

"Remember my stories and all the characters I have created. Each shared a part of my soul and heart. They were a part of me.

"I never betrayed any of them in wanting to live, but able to face death when it was inevitable.

"A fear of living and a fear of dying.

"That's who I was and ended up to be.

"My epitaph, Mr. Perkins."

Perkins looked toward Fitzgerald.

"A hard one to follow, Hemingway, as you have always been so eloquent and bold. It's hard to follow you after you have entered a room." Fitzgerald smiled, as did Hemingway. "But I shall try.

"Whose headstone shall be read the most, anyway?"

All in the room broke into a hilarious roar.

"I chide you, Hemingway, as you have me over the years of our friendship."

"Well done, and I shall remember it all of my eternal life.

"I wish I had written more and dallied less. I can't change that now.

"I was knighted, 'The Jazz Age Writer.' Perfect for the era, but it confined my scope of creativity.

"My epitaph: 'Born with a talent to write that was never fully developed.'

"Already, on my tombstone appear the words: 'So, we beat on, boats against the current, borne back ceaselessly into the past.'

"From *The Great Gatsby*.

"That surmises my life."

O. Henry went next.

"My legacy is simple. He wrote honestly, with a pen connected to his heart.

"As Dickens has said, listen with your ears and your heart. Neither of them lies.

"I want my legacy to reflect my love for the people, especially the downtrodden, for surely, they are blessed more than you and me. I never wrote for fame, only to reflect love and human kindness, which seems to be distant nowadays.

"Please write my name on my grave as 'William Sydney Porter.' I am not ashamed but only proud of what I have accomplished and who I am.

"That is enough for my epitaph."

Dickens was the last of the four to speak.

"My legacy would be to remember me as a true and sincere author.

"A descriptive writer that engaged you in the story and made my characters come alive. As real as if they were standing before you.

"I am often referred to as a writer of classical novels."
"That I will gladly leave as my legacy and my epitaph."

Farewell

The sun started to rise on the edge of the eastern sky. Light began to filter through the door into the room.

A rooster crowed.

There was a pause. The conversation halted.

Maxwell made notice.

"Gentlemen…I believe our time has run out. I hope this meeting of the minds was worth your effort.

"I did not wish to invade your privacy or disturb your peaceful rest.

"I thought it would be good for us to purge our souls and share the wealth of our talent; our dreams, successes, and failures; to share and encourage all writers who will follow us.

"The world needs you now, even more so than when you were alive."

"My final question to all. What would be your advice to new, aspiring writers?

"Be brief as our time wanes.

The master of prose spoke first. Dickens.

"The world of words takes precedence over everything else. You can live in neither the past nor the future. Learn to intertwine the two into the present.

"Trust it, and let it go. Write more and without remorse. Not all will believe in you.

"Believe in yourself.

"As far as advice, never underestimate the power of observation. Many of my characters came to life with a mixture of all the people that entered and left my world. Names, subtle habits; how someone sneezed, hobbled, walked or behaved, ate. All were important.

"Study the people around you; the events happening at the time. Even the environment."

"Those were the roots of all my stories. Observation can be your best friend, along with your imagination.

"That's where all of my stories began and ended.

"One last bit of advice, if you please, gentlemen.

"If you are happy in your life as it is, stay there. Never venture further than your front door. But you will never find new horizons or new stories by staying home."

Hemingway spoke up.

"Dickens, you are just and kind.

"Future authors, know yourself well.

"Be bold and speak for yourself. The words you write are your own. If you write it, believe it.

"Never apologize for the stories you have created.

"They are honest and true from your heart.

"Be strong, by God, finish it. Never moon over the last story. Write more and with even more zest and enthusiasm than before.

"Never let a bad review throw you. Critics know little or even less than you do about humanity and even less about your heart, or story.

"Move on."

O. Henry was next to speak.

"Gentlemen, those were true and honest observations; I must deviate a bit.

"Even though we think of writing for ourselves. The story

would be meaningless without the reader. In all my stories, I put the reader first. I needed to touch an emotion or a heart.

"Sensitivity, reality, and the ability for my reader to experience the story firsthand."

"Otherwise, why should they even read it at all.

"No. My advice is to not find self-preservation, but to move human emotion forward, finding victory in even our greatest losses.

"Words have power. They can be destructive or a balm in one's simple mind.

"Write with clarity, compassion, and understanding. Always put yourself in the position of your reader.

"Know in your heart; they will relate and sleep well in knowing you have made their world a better place.

"Write with a pure and clear soul."

Fitzgerald went last.

"First of all, know your characters; know their strengths and weaknesses. Know them as well as you know yourself.

"Know the subject matter and the circumstances. Have a gripping beginning and an idea for the ending; fill the story with adversity and victory, even if it's tragic.

"As my fellow authors mentioned, always believe in yourself first.

"You'll sometimes write yourself into a corner. Figure it out or rewrite it. There will be many times when you will need to change direction. It's okay; that's the exciting part of writing. You can change the outcome or what you want to happen.

"It's your story, but let the characters tell you what to write and how to get to where they want you to go.

"Listen to them."

Perkins proceeded to bring the meeting to a conclusion.

"Well-versed, gentlemen, and great advice from all. As an

editor and a publisher, I have worked with many writers, and the words that were spoken tonight stand true and pass the test of time.

"Thank you for your participation, honesty, and truthfulness.

"May this help to prepare new writers for our prestigious guild.

"I believe we will meet again soon.

"Perhaps others will join us at another time.

Fitzgerald, Hemingway, O. Henry, and Dickens nodded in unison. Handshakes and smiles were exchanged.

The room darkened briefly, and when the sun rose and the fog lifted, the café was empty.